Three Little Beavers

by Jean Heilprin Diehl

illustrated by Cathy Morrison

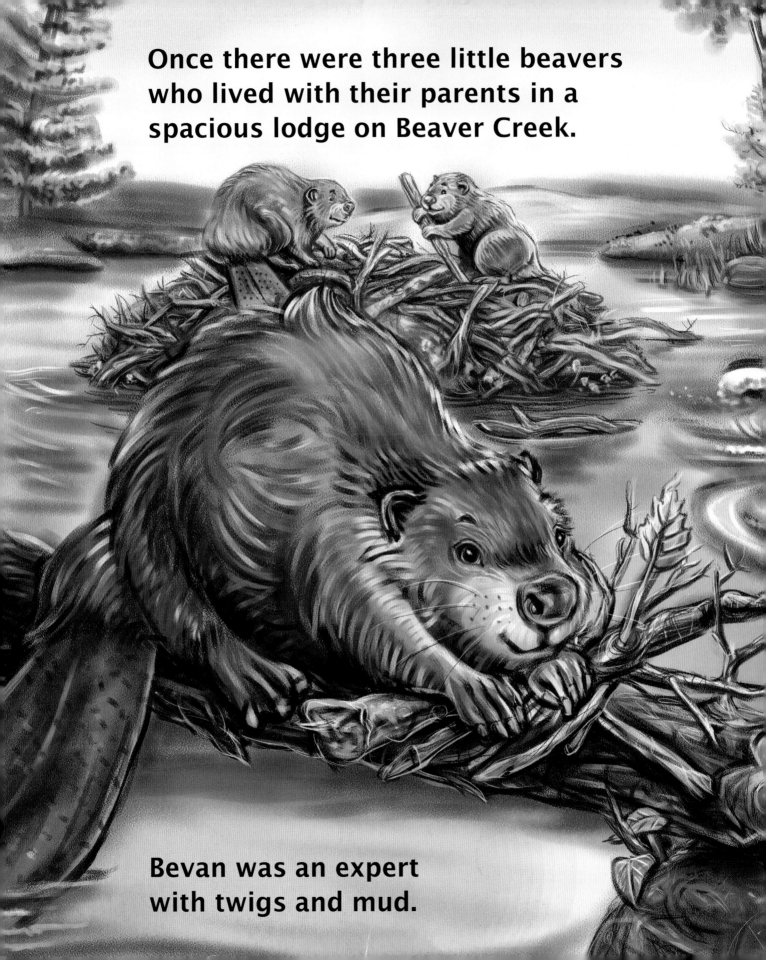

Once there were three little beavers who lived with their parents in a spacious lodge on Beaver Creek.

Bevan was an expert with twigs and mud.

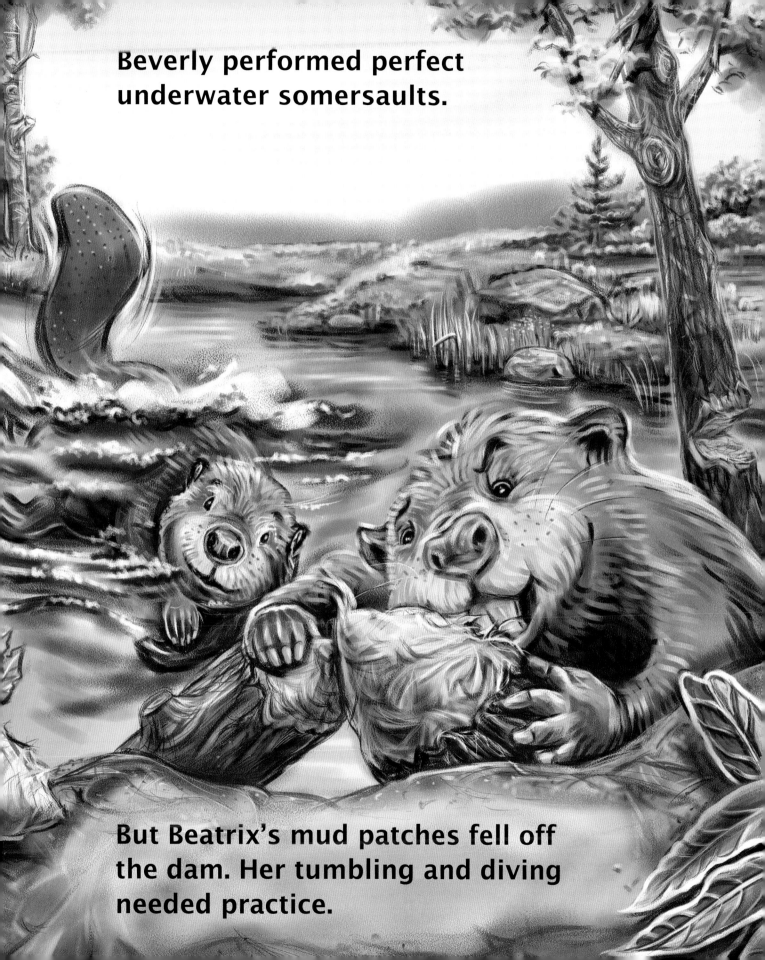

Beverly performed perfect underwater somersaults.

But Beatrix's mud patches fell off the dam. Her tumbling and diving needed practice.

All summer long, Beatrix did her best to gnaw trees and stash branches to store food for winter. She tried to mend the lodge and the dam. She dug a canal, sort of. Something always seemed to go wrong.

Meanwhile, Bevan and Beverly seemed to do everything perfectly.

What am I good at? Beatrix wondered. One evening, she swam away up Beaver Creek to find out. A river otter scared her, but she swam around it.

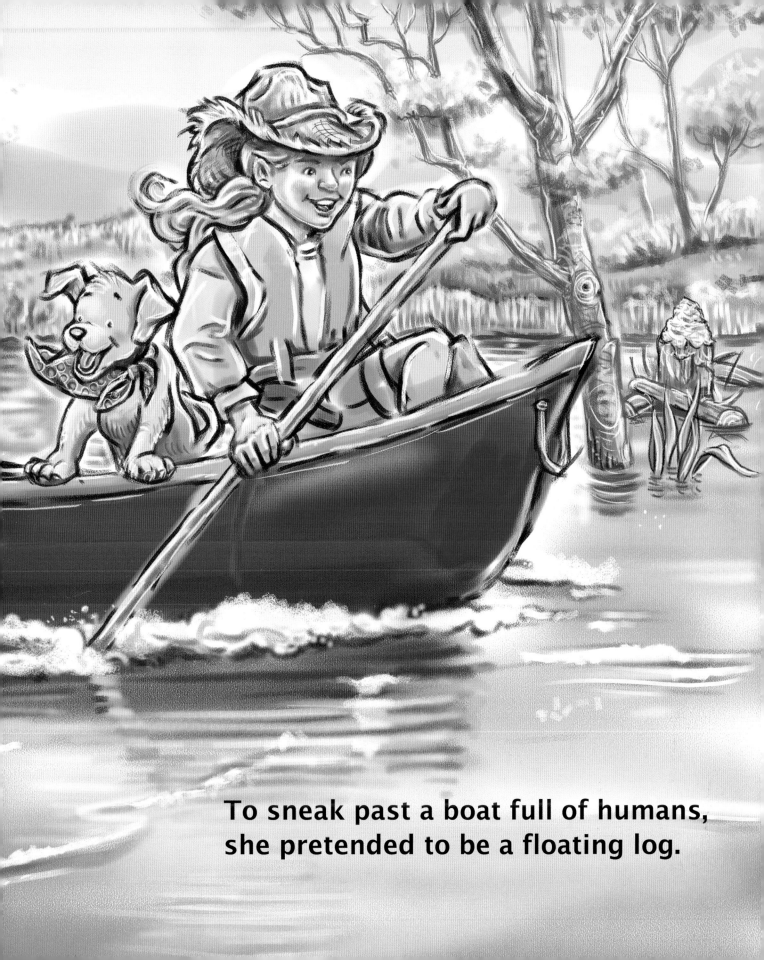

To sneak past a boat full of humans, she pretended to be a floating log.

Beatrix climbed into a grassy meadow. She scuttled and hopped past low, funny-looking trees too dry to eat. She chewed a thin aspen trunk and skittered out of the way in time for the timber to fall. By moonlight, Beatrix nibbled the tender shoots and tasty bark. Then she snacked on nearby berries.

Near the water grew a delicious-looking clump of clover. As she reached for it—*whap!*—a box-shaped trap slapped shut around her.

Beatrix watched the creek flow by, toward the dam and home. She stayed calm and alert, ready for whatever would happen next.

Where was Beatrix? Her parents searched the woods and the canals. Bevan and Beverly swam up the creek.

Beverly was so excited to find Beatrix that she turned somersaults until—*whap*—a trap caught her, too.

Bevan chopped down a young willow. As he pushed branches into the cages to give his sisters something to eat, he slipped and found himself—*whap*—in trap number three.

Beverly tumbled nervously inside her box until she cut her tail on a sharp edge.

Bevan gnawed a metal bar until he chipped a tooth. Terrified, he quaked in a corner.

But Beatrix was quiet. She watched and waited.

Seeing their sister, Bevan and Beverly felt better. They grew quiet, too.

At dawn, people appeared.

They lifted the three traps and set them facing each other on the grass. Beverly threw herself against the metal sides. Bevan huddled with fright. But Beatrix stayed curious and levelheaded. So Bevan and Beverly relaxed a little, too.

"We need to move these beavers far away, to a new pond, where they can't destroy our plants."

"But they might not do well in a new home."

"What's the use of moving them? More beavers will come in their place."

"Excuse me, I'm a guest here. I came to the inn hoping to see beavers. I have an idea . . ."

Then, hammering and sawing started. Beatrix usually slept during the day, but there was too much noise for that now. Someone shoved a branch into her cage: *Bleh!* Oak leaves, not what she liked to eat.

Hours went by, until *Creak!* The door to Beatrix's cage lifted. *Creak! Creak!* Bevan and Beverly's cages opened, too. Bevan and Beverly were too scared to move, until they saw Beatrix.

She lumbered into the sunlight, happy and hungry. Low fences now ringed the delicious trees and gardens. Beatrix led her brother and sister down the bank to the creek, where the three little beavers feasted on lily tubers and pondweeds . . .

Beaver Safari:
Nightly Boat Tour to a real beaver lodge: 7 pm

. . . until several guests from the inn approached, with cameras.

Beverly dove underwater with fright. Bevan snapped a stalk in two and froze. But Beatrix slapped her tail on the water and led the three little beavers as they swam away home.

For Creative Minds

Beaver Fun Facts and Adaptations

All living things have adaptations that allow them to live in their habitat. Some of those adaptations are body parts and some are behaviors. Beaver adaptations help them to live in and around water.

Beavers are the largest rodents in North America. An adult beaver's tail is about 12 inches (30 cm) long. Including the tail, a beaver can be up to four feet (1.2 m) and weigh as much as 70 lbs. (31 kg). How tall are you and how much do you weigh? How does that compare to an adult beaver?

American beavers live near rivers, streams, ponds, lakes, and marshes. They are slow moving on land but are graceful and fast swimming in the water.

They live all over North America except for Florida, the deserts of the US Southwest and Mexico, or the very northern part of Canada and Alaska.

Busy as a beaver . . . beavers spend much of their time looking for food, knocking down trees, building or repairing their lodges or dams. They are most active at night (nocturnal).

Beavers living in cold climates will store food underwater for the winter near their home.

Beavers eat the inner bark and leaves of some trees. Because they can't reach the leaves or high bark, they chop the trees down. They also use the wood from felled trees to build dams and lodges.

They will also eat some flowers and plants.

When swimming, special "valves" on the nose (nostrils), ears, and back of the throat close so beavers can carry sticks in their mouths.

Beavers mark their territory with scents.

Because they use their tail and back feet to swim, they can carry things when they swim.

They slap their tails on the water to warn other beavers of danger.

Young are born in the spring and are called "kits."

Their front feet are like hands and are used to hold things and dig.

Humans have adaptations too. Our hands have opposable thumbs to pick up and hold onto objects. We make and use things to make up for body parts we don't have. Can you match the objects we use to the beaver adaptations? Use the images below to answer the questions. Answers are upside down, below.

 **eyes**: Beavers have a clear cover (called nictitating membrane) over their eyes so they can see while underwater. What do we use to see underwater?

 **feet**: Their big back feet are webbed for swimming. What do we use on our feet to help us swim?

The 4th toe on each back foot is split and is used to comb their fur.

 **fur**: Like many mammals, beavers have two layers of fur: long, thick waterproof "guard" hair (that's what we see) and a layer of short, soft underfur for warmth. What do we use to stay warm and dry in cold weather?

 **tail**: Beavers use their tails to warn of danger and to steer and push through the water (like a rudder). They also use it like a "kickstand" to balance when cutting down trees, to store fat, and have sweat glands. What do we use to steer and push a boat through the water?

 **teeth**: Long front teeth are used for gnawing on and cutting down trees. The teeth are constantly growing but the gnawing keeps them from growing too long. What do we use to cut down trees or to cut wood?

Answers: eyes: swim goggles; feet: swim flippers; fur: a coat, sweater, or jacket; tail: a paddle; teeth: a saw

Hands On: Lodges and Dams

Using sticks, branches, grass, rocks, and mud, beavers build homes, called lodges, on the shoreline or in the middle of a lake or pond.

The lodges usually have two underwater entrances, to help beavers stay away from predators. If a predator comes in one entrance, the beavers can leave through the other. The living area stays warm and dry since it is higher than the water level. The living area is about 8 feet (2.4 m) wide and is lined with bark and grass. Beavers leave a hole in the ceiling so fresh air can come in.

The only other animals that change their environment more than beavers are humans or elephants. Beavers change woodlands into wetlands and elephants change woodlands into grasslands.

If the water around their lodge or den is not deep enough, beavers will build dams out of the same materials as their lodges. The dams block the water flow, raising the water level, making new beaver ponds. Ponds are safer for the beavers to get away from land-based predators. Beavers also dig canals to make it easier to get in and out of the lodge.

Since beavers are slow moving on land, the higher level of the new pond and the canals make it easier for the beavers to reach trees for food and building materials. Beavers would much rather haul branches by swimming than by walking through the woods!

Beaver ponds become home to many wetland animals and migrating birds. As long as the beavers live in the area, they will repair the dam if it breaks or leaks. After beavers leave the area, the ponds often turn into meadows and then forests, changing the animal habitat again.

Build Your Own Beaver Dam

Find and gather sticks, twigs, rocks, pebbles, and dirt from your yard. If gathering from someone else's yard or property, make sure to ask permission first.

Find a long, deep container or pan.

Use your gathered materials to build a dam going through the middle of the container.

Pour water into the container on one side.

Does your dam hold the water back?

If not, how can you fix it so the water is blocked from getting to the other side?

Busy Beavers: Pests or Environmental Engineers?

Beavers are engineers—they change their environment through their work.

Some people think that beavers are pests because the beavers change people's land.

Other people like the way beavers create wetlands used by many other animals and plants.

What do YOU think?

> Are these beaver behaviors good or bad from a human point of view?
>
> What about other animals?
>
> Which human behaviors prevent beavers from damaging property?

A pair of beavers can cut down up to 400 trees every year. Trees felled by beavers can damage buildings or fences.

Many people live near the rivers and streams that the beavers dam. Roads or people's backyards can disappear under the beaver ponds.

Beavers create ponds, wetlands, and new-growth forests that become habitats for many other animals. Because so many other animals rely on these habitats, beavers are said to be a "keystone species." If the beavers aren't there, the other animals won't be either.

Beaver ponds act as sponges to absorb sediments or pollution running off the land from farming, logging, or mining.

Some people set traps on their land for beavers. Once trapped, the beavers are sometimes moved to another location and let go.

People put up fences so the beavers can't get into yards or around individual trees. Some people use piping systems to control the water level in a beaver pond. The pipes let the water get deep enough for the beavers but not deep enough to flood.

For Sandy and Caroline—JHD

To my "BFF" Ginny, who's "busy as a beaver" yet always there for me—CM

Thanks to Sheila Cohen, Visitor Use Assistant at Prince William Forest Park; Oklahoma Aquarium educators Ann Money and Michelle Zarantonello; and beaver experts Dr. Steve Windels and Tawnya Schoewe for reviewing the accuracy of the information in this book.

Library of Congress Cataloging-in-Publication Data

Diehl, Jean Heilprin.
  Three little beavers / by Jean Heilprin Diehl ; illustrated by Cathy Morrison.
    p. cm.
  Summary: Feeling less gifted than her older sister Beverly and older brother Bevan, Beatrix the beaver discovers her true talents when the three siblings are caught in human traps.
  ISBN 978-1-60718-524-6 (hardcover) -- ISBN 978-1-60718-533-8 (pbk.) -- ISBN 978-1-60718-542-0 (english ebook) -- ISBN 978-1-60718-551-2 (spanish ebook) [1. Beavers--Fiction.] I. Morrison, Cathy, ill. II. Title.
  PZ7.D5725Th 2012
  [E]--dc23
                          2011044225

Also available as eBooks featuring auto-flip, auto-read, 3D-page-curling, and selectable English and Spanish text and audio
Interest level: 004-008   Grade level: P-3   Lexile® Level: 630L Lexile® Code: AD
Curriculum keywords: adaptations, anthropomorphic, change environment, individual differences, life science: general, water features (ocean, lakes, ponds, wetlands, rivers)

Manufactured in China, December, 2011
This product conforms to CPSIA 2008
First Printing
Sylvan Dell Publishing
Mt. Pleasant, SC 29464